Angel John & Nano

ON VACATION

Guardian Angels Series vol.2

Written by:
Mireille Mishriky

Illustrated by:
Luis Baeza

Do you know how Angel John and Baby Nano met? Get your copy of the first book in the Guardian Angels Series!

3

Nano is getting ready to travel with her family. It will be the first time she goes on a plane. Her mom shows her a picture of a plane and pointed out the wings that would make the plane fly, like Angel John's wings.

Angel John has been caring for Nano since she was a baby, and he was by her side as she blew out the four candles on her birthday cake last Sunday.

5

Nano and her family attend liturgy, have communion, and then Nano and Angel John attend Sunday School class. She sits on a small chair, and he hovers next to her.

The Sunday School teacher distributes pictures for the children to colour. It was a picture of a Guardian Angel watching over a young girl and boy beside a river. Angel John has a big smile as he watches Nano colour in the image and wonders if she realizes how he is also protecting her day and night.

Not just at rivers, on the street, or in a car. Not just from physical danger and harm. Angel John, like all Guardian Angels, is there to help children as they grow in their spiritual life as well.

For example, now that Nano is going on her first vacation, Angel John will make sure that she remembers to pray before bedtime and when she wakes up.

Nano looks through her closet and pulls out all the clothes she wants to pack in her bag. She gets up on the step stool and reaches for a hanger when the chair nearly topples over. Thank God for Angel John, who quickly slides his wing beneath the chair to steady it!

While packing her suitcase, Nano makes space for her stuffed bunny, her hairbrush, and her sun hat. As she is about to close her bag, Angel John opens the window above Nano's bedside table, making Nano turn around and realize that she had forgotten to pack her book of Bible stories. Travelling away from home does not mean travelling without our Bible, thinks Angel John.

Once she packs her book of Bible stories, Nano closes her suitcase, puts it by her bedroom door and gets ready for bed.

Angel John watches as she brushes her teeth, kisses her parents goodnight, and settles in her big girl's bed. Before she closes her eyes, Angel John quickly whispers in her heart that she has forgotten to pray.

Nano promptly gets out of bed and bends on her knees to say her prayers. There is always time for worship, and Angel John finds new ways to remind Nano about her prayers every morning, every night and before every meal.

The big day is finally here! Nano is climbing the steps and about to enter the airplane that will carry her and her parents to their beach vacation. Angel John watches as Nano buckles her seat belt and opens the airplane window. As the plane is getting ready for take-off, Angel John prays for Nano's safety and settles on top of her seat. He knows he will have to be extra careful over the following days.

Because, even though Nano is going on vacation, Angel John and all Guardian Angels never do! They are always there, watching over their children and protecting them from physical and spiritual harm.

Angel John watches Nano's eyes stare at the ocean. She has never seen an ocean before. Angel John notices how she is overwhelmed by its size and wonders if she realizes that Jesus' love for her is even larger than all the oceans combined.

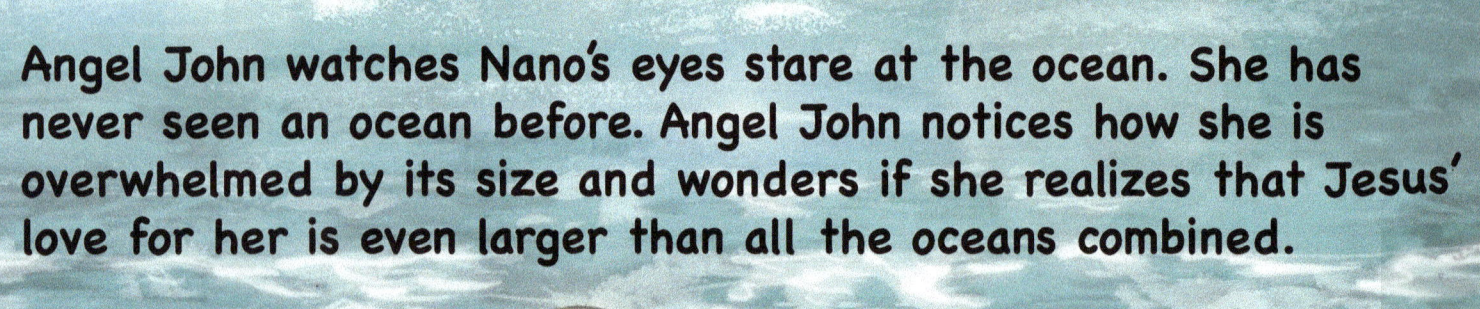

Nano grasps her mother's hand and takes her first step on the hot sand. Then, step by step, Nano nears the water as the small waves are bringing seashells to the shore. But not just seashells; there are jellyfish riding the small waves.

Jellyfish are almost transparent and very difficult to spot. While they are gorgeous to behold, their sting is very painful! In a flash, Angel John twirls the oncoming wave with his wings and sends the jellyfish back to the ocean, far away from Nano and any other child.

Splish splash! Nano is having a blast in the sea. The small waves tickle her toes, and she gathers as many seashells as her small chubby hands can: a pink seashell, a brown one, and a cream one shaped like an ice cream cone.

Because Nano is busy collecting seashells, she does not realize that a gigantic wave is heading her way. However, because Angel John's eyes are constantly focusing on Nano, he rushes to her rescue. He positions himself between her and the wave and covers her with his wings. If it were not for Angel John, Nano would have been swept under the tide!

As the sun sets, Nano packs her seashell collection in her yellow bucket and heads toward her parents' beach chairs. She is eager to show them all the colorful seashells she gathered on her first day at the beach and does not want to drop any. Unfortunately, she is so focused on her collection that she does not see the small piece of broken glass on the sand and steps on it, hurting her foot. Angel John prays for Nano as her parents rush to her side, clean the cut and put a band-aid on her heel.

Angel John's prayers, like those of our Guardian Angels, help us when bad things happen. We should never be afraid because, unlike us, Guardian Angels never go on vacation and are always watching over us.